This book belongs to

....

....

Crazy Creepy Crawlie

For Tom, Sandy, Bonnie and Alex Holmes – KP
For Amy, Tom, Bill and Lucia – RC

Published by **KAMA** Publishing
19A The Swale, Norwich, NR5 9HE
www.kamapublishing.co.uk

First printed 2012

Text © Kevin Price,
Illustrations © Robin Carter

British Library Cataloguing in Publication Data. A catalogue record for this book is available from the British Library.

Paperback ISBN 9780956719638

Printed in Great Britain by
Barnwell Print Ltd, Dunkirk, Aylsham, Norfolk. NR11 6SU

WORLD LAND TRUST™
www.carbonbalancedpaper.com
CBP000128310002123442

By using Carbon Balanced Paper through the World Land Trust on this publication we have saved 1175kg of Carbon & preserved 99sqm of critically threatened tropical forests.

Carbon Balanced Paper. One of the most sustainable forms of communication that will reduce your carbon foot print and promote CSR. www.carbonbalancepaper.com

Crazy creepy Crawlies

by Kevin Price

Illustrated by Robin Carter

Belligerent Bees

The worker Bees cried, "How would you lot survive

If we didn't bring nectar back to the hive?

We're calling a strike, we're demanding more money,

You'd better pay up or you won't get your honey!"

Caterpillar Chaos

Carly the Caterpillar won't learn to fly

Until she turns into a big butterfly,

But that didn't stop her from having a bash;

She jumped off a leaf.......

.......and fell down with a crash!

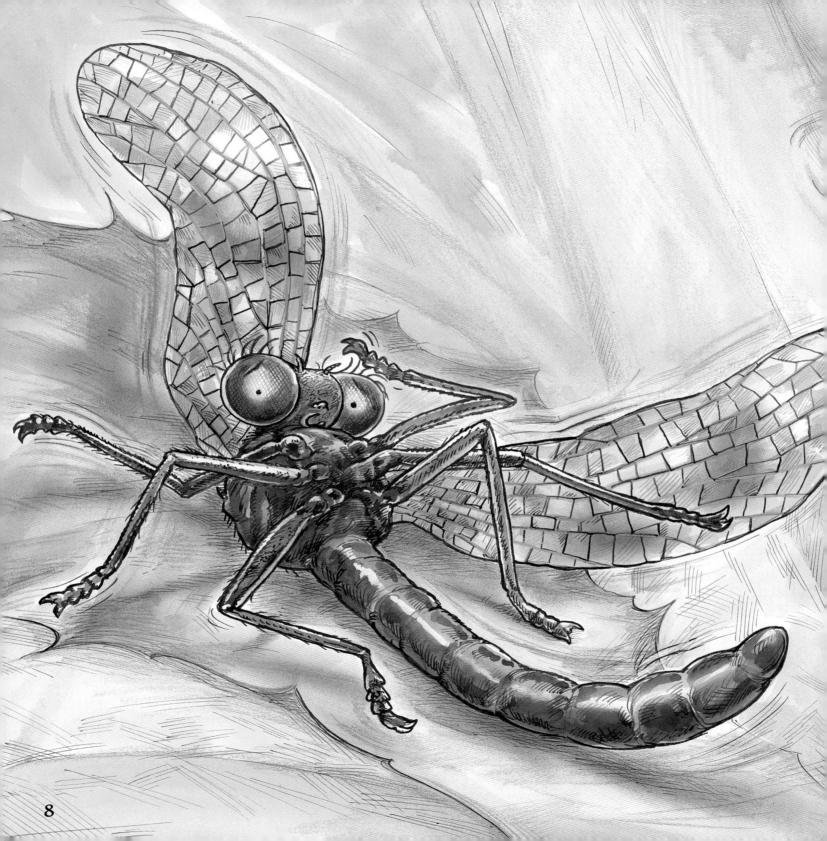

Damselfly's Dance

When Daphne the Damselfly dances and sings

She keeps tripping over her lovely long wings.

She's found a solution, though it wasn't planned;

Her wings got caught up in her spangly hair band!

An Ode to Dung Beetles

I wouldn't like to be a Dung Beetle, would you?

They spend their whole lives munching elephant poo,

And they really love it; to them it's a treat,

But I know there's much nicer things they could eat!

Earwig Emergency

Ernie the Earwig nipped me with his pincers.

I shouted, "I'd like to put you through a mincer!"

I yelled and I cursed at that horrible bug,

But he didn't care – he just gave a shrug.

Flippin' Flies

Francis the Fly isn't really so bad,

But flies round my head and that drives me quite mad.

When I've had enough and can't take any more

I slip off my shoe and swish him through the door.

15

Lazy Ladybird?

Lottie the Ladybird's feeling unwell;

"I can't go to school Mum, I don't feel so swell.

First I get chilly and then I get hot;

And look Mum, just look – I've come out in spots!"

Shoe Saga

Millie the Millipede was facing defeat;

She just couldn't find enough shoes for her feet.

But she smiled when the postman delivered a box –

Her Granny had knitted a thousand pink socks.

Moth's Marathon

When Maurice the Moth emerged from his cocoon,

He flew round our lamp, which he thought was the moon.

Then two hours later he gave out a shout,

"I need to lie down, I'm completely puffed out!"

Spider's Snack

Sylvester the Spider was at a low ebb

Until something tasty got caught in his web.

He's eating his lunch now, would you like to t

He's just tucking into a fat, juicy fly.

Wasp Warning

If Willie the Wasp gets upset then he'll sting

And I have to warn you, it's not a nice thing!

It throbs and it tingles, it causes great pain;

I'm not going to swat Willie ever again!

Woodworm's Woe

Walter the Woodworm was seeking a home.

He walked a long way, far and wide he did roam.

He thought an oak table would be quite fantastic,

But kept finding furniture made out of plastic.

Crazy creepy Crawlies

supports

WORLD
LAND
TRUST

WORLD LAND TRUST

Saving Real Acres in Real Places

The World Land Trust believes that all creatures have their place on our planet. It isn't just about saving the big animals like Tigers, Elephants and the Giant Panda, it is about saving the whole habitat for all the animals that live in it. Just as important as the animals we know about are the birds and insects that make up the 'web of life' in a habitat. Each one has its role to play. It is generally believed that if all insects were to disappear humans wouldn't be able to survive for more than a few months. And most other animals - amphibians, reptiles, birds and mammals - would also become extinct because of the domino effect that would happen in the food chain. World Land Trust saves whole habitats for all wildlife … and humans.

Message from Sir David Attenborough

"The only way to save the Tiger or the Elephant is to save the habitat in which it lives because there's a mutual dependency between them and millions of other species of both animals and plants. It is that range of biodiversity that we must care for—the whole thing—rather than just one or two stars."

Sir David Attenborough, Patron World Land Trust

World Land Trust is even saving the habitat of the most poisonous vertebrate on Earth!

Deep in the heart of the Colombian rainforests lives the Golden Poison Frog, *Phyllobates terribilis*, one of the most awe-inspiring species known to mankind and the most poisonous vertebrate on Earth. Just 55mm in length, this tiny creature carries enough poison to kill about 10 humans, with just a single milligram of toxin. The frog's skin is drenched in a poison which, if it comes into contact with human skin leads to heart failure and death within minutes. The indigenous people of the forests in Colombia have used the lethal poison of the frog for centuries. The Choco Emberā Indians would gently brush the tips of the arrows and darts on the frog's back (which causes it no harm), making the weapon deadly for more than two years afterwards. But even the frog's deadly poison cannot protect it from the threat of humans. It lives in a small area of tropical forest which is threatened by logging and mining and if the forests were to disappear so would the frogs. The World Land Trust believes it is essential that the awesome Golden Poison Frog survives in the wild.

What do these big words mean?

Golden Poison Frog

Habitats: A habitat consists of all the kinds of plants that grow there, the animals that live there, the climate and the geography. Examples of habitats include Rainforest, Grasslands, Coral Reefs

Biodiversity: Is a single word to describe the range of plants and animals that live in a habitat.

Invertebrates: Animals without a backbone—such as spiders, slugs and snails.

Vertebrate: All things that have a backbone, so this includes humans, cats and dogs, and also big wild animals, such as tigers, elephants and monkeys, and also smaller creatures such as frogs and lizards.

30

Some wild and wonderful facts about "Creepy Crawlies"

- In every square mile of habitable land on the planet there are thought to be over 25,000 million insects.
- At the last count there were thought to be more than 35,000 species of spiders, but scientists are still counting.
- Up to 30 metres of silk (nearly 100 feet) goes into a garden spider's web.
- The world's largest spider is the Goliath Bird-eating Spider (a South American tarantula) with a body length of 3.5 inches, a leg span of 11 inches and fangs measuring one inch long.
- The largest beetle is now known to be the Titan Beetle that lives in the Amazon. It grows up to seven inches long.
- Able to fly at over 35 mph, dragonflies are the world's fastest flyers.
- Desert locusts form swarms of over 50 billion individuals.
- The Velvet Worm, found in many countries in the southern hemisphere, can squirt glue, just like Spiderman.
- A 500g jar of honey represents about ten million trips from the hive to flowers and back again by worker bees.

The World Land Trust was established in 1989 to protect critically threatened habitats for their wildlife. So far over 500,000 acres have been saved throughout the world and are now protected by local organisations as nature reserves.

All donations resulting from the sale of this book will be used by World Land Trust and its overseas project partners to purchase threatened tropical forest to create more reserves thereby ensuring the survival of all the species that live in them.

A donation will save Real Acres in Real Places

World Land Trust is a registered charity No. 1001291
Its Patrons are Sir David Attenborough and David Gower

For information or a School Pack please contact:

World Land Trust, Blyth House, Bridge Street,
Halesworth, Suffolk IP19 8AB
Telephone: 01986 874 422

www.worldlandtrust.org

The images of the insects on this page were taken on the Reserva Ecológica de Guapi Assu (REGUA) Reserve in Brazil, some of the last remaining Atlantic Rainforest. World Land Trust works closely with REGUA and has so far funded the purchase of 18,000 acres (7,400 hectares) of tropical forest, which is now protected as a nature reserve. Small numbers of visitors are encouraged and these images were taken by Chris Knowles from the UK.